TO SOPHIE-LAURE B.

Text and Illustrations © 2022 Barroux

Published in Great Britain in 2022 by Otter-Barry Books, Little Orchard,
Burley Gate, Herefordshire, HR1 3QS. www.otterbarrybooks.com

Published in the United States of America and Canada in 2022 by Flyaway Books,
100 Witherspoon Street, Louisville, Kentucky 40202-1396. www.flyawaybooks.com

22 23 24 25 26 27 28 29 30 31–10 9 8 7 6 5 4 3 2 1

Book design by Allison Taylor
Text set in Supernett cn

Library of Congress Cataloging-in-Publication Data is on file at the Library of Congress, Washington, DC.

ISBN: 9781947888364

PRINTED IN CHINA

Most Flyaway Books are available at special quantity discounts when purchased
in bulk by corporations, organizations, and special-interest groups.
For more information, please e-mail SpecialSales@flyawaybooks.com.

I LOVE YOU, BLUE

art and story by

BARROUX

I LOVE THE BLUE OF THE OCEAN.

BUT TODAY THE SKY TURNS GRAY.

THE OCEAN ROARS AND RAGES.

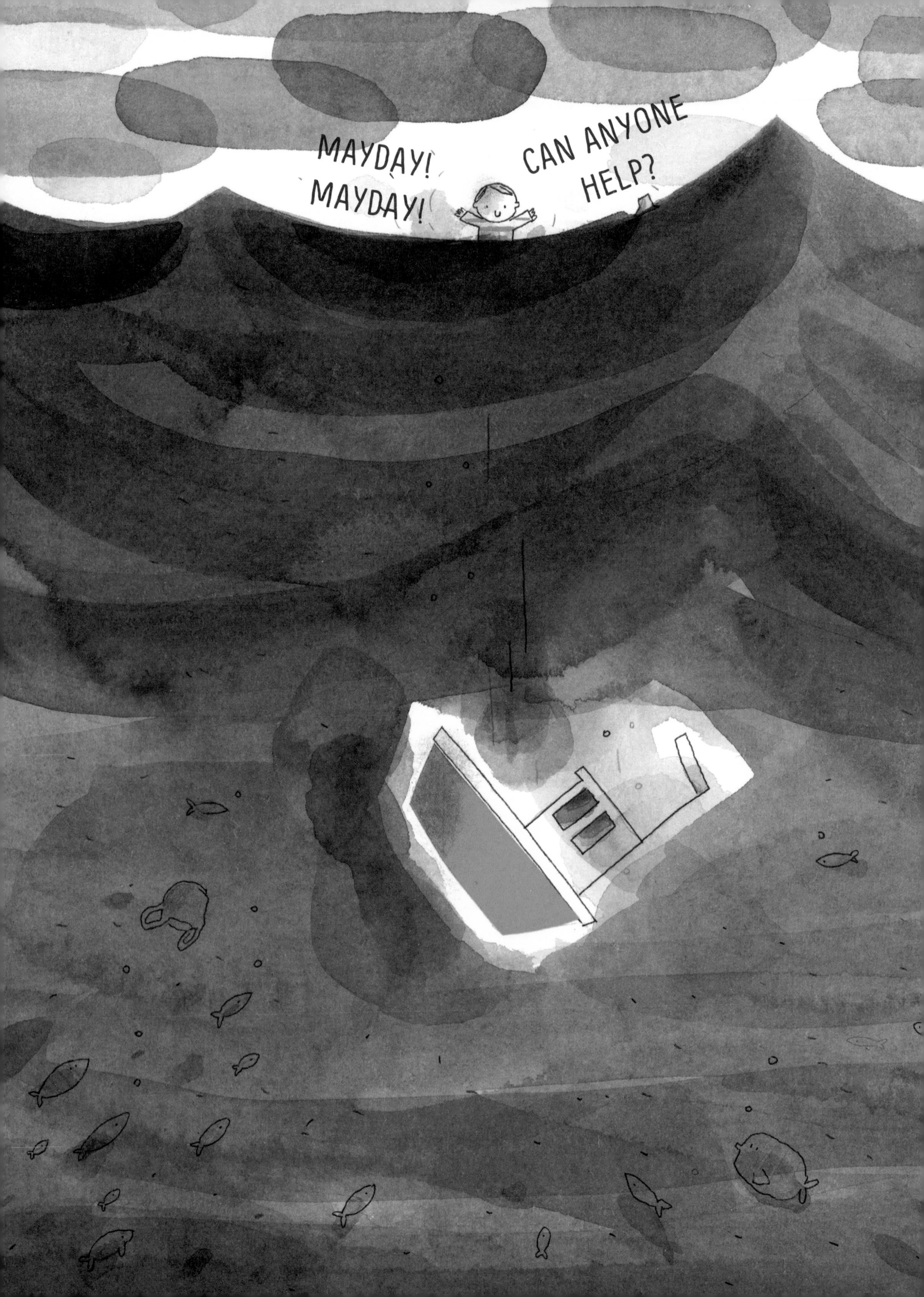
MAYDAY!
MAYDAY!
CAN ANYONE
HELP?

THANK YOU!
YOU SAVED MY BOAT—
AND MY LIFE!

WHAT'S YOUR NAME?

BLUE.

BLUE, THANK YOU AGAIN.
I HOPE I WILL SEE YOU TOMORROW.

BLUE, BLUE . . .

YOU ARE BEAUTIFUL.

BLUE, BLUE . . .

GOOD NIGHT.

TRA LA LA! IT'S A LOVELY NEW DAY.

HERE I COME, BLUE!

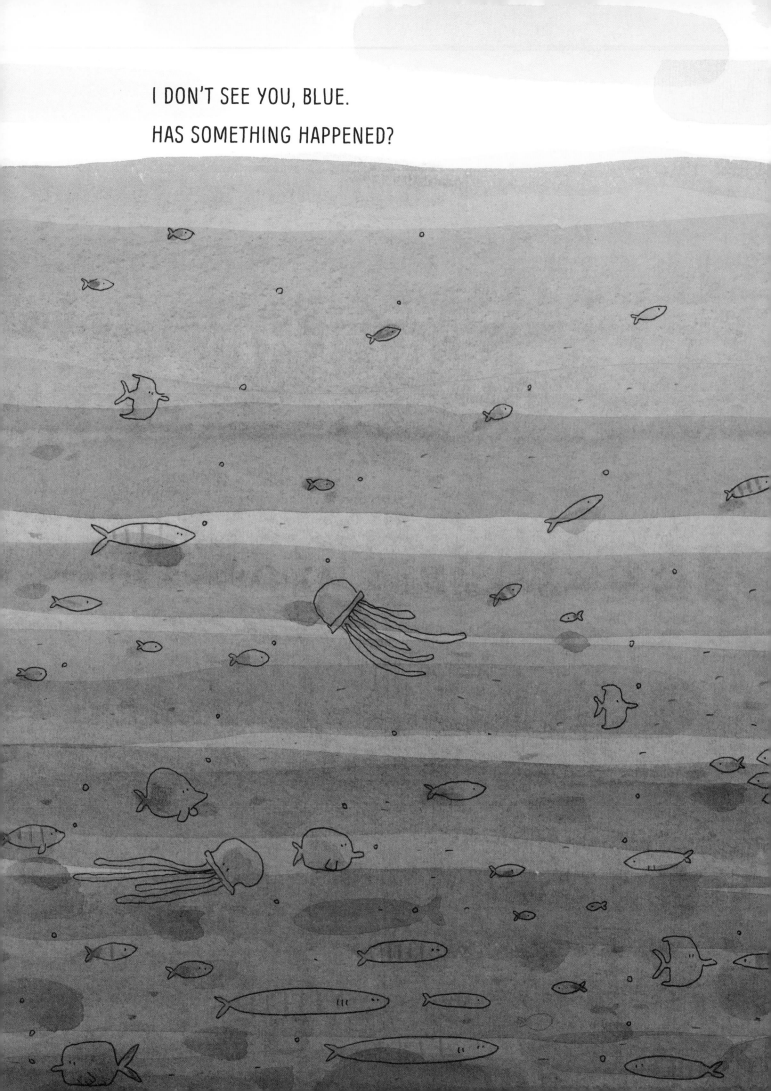

I DON'T SEE YOU, BLUE.

HAS SOMETHING HAPPENED?

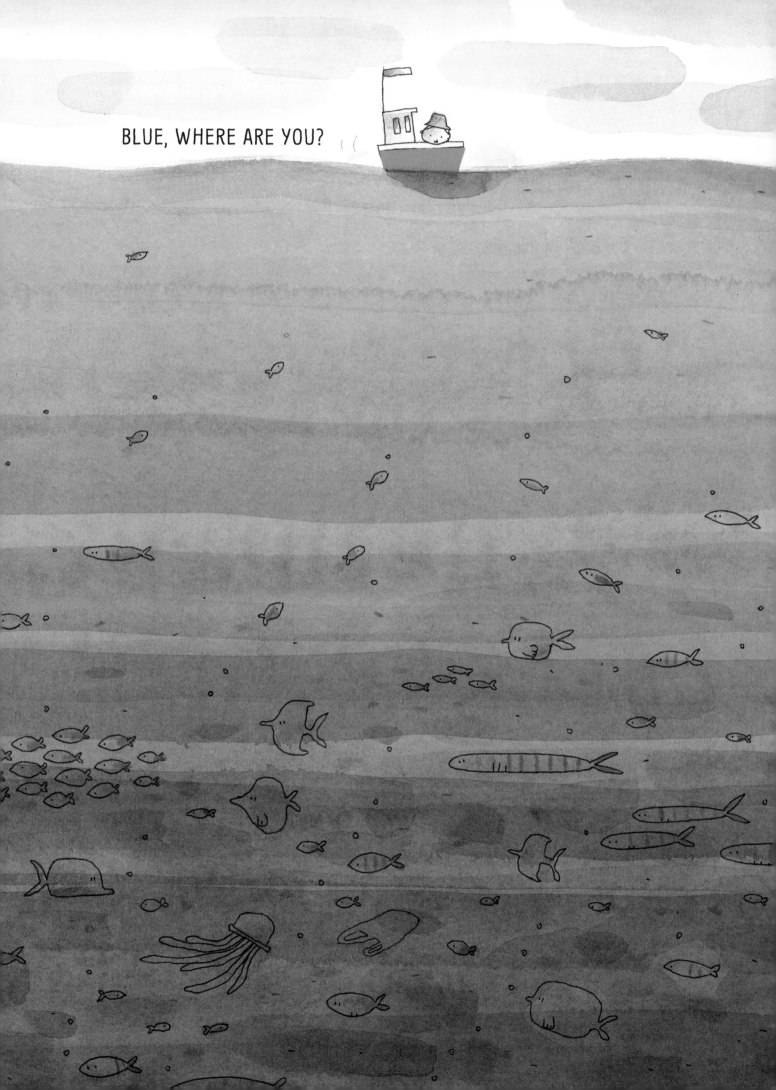

BLUE, WHERE ARE YOU?

OH, BLUE, THERE YOU ARE!

YOU DON'T LOOK WELL.

DO YOU FEEL SICK?

OPEN YOUR MOUTH AND SAY, "AAAH."

LET'S GET RID OF ALL THIS TRASH.

I HOPE YOU WILL FEEL MUCH BETTER.

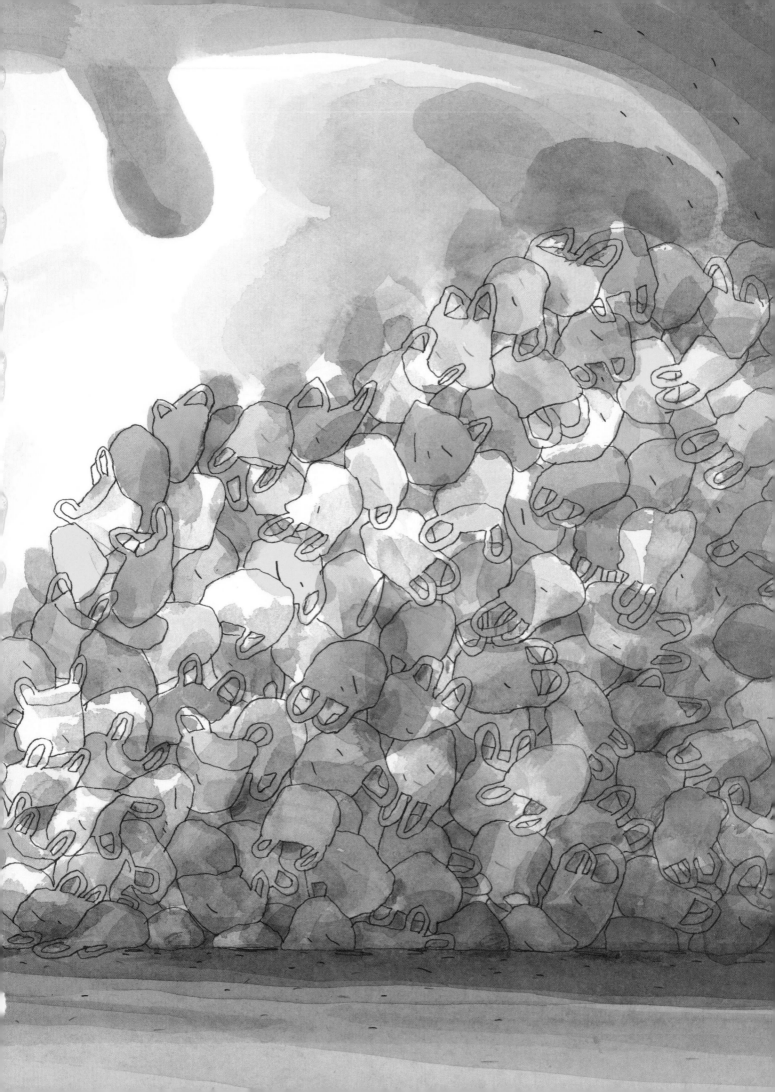

WOW! IT'S HUGE IN HERE.

POOR BLUE!
NO WONDER YOU'RE SICK.
YOU HAVE A BELLY FULL OF BAGS!

I'M TAKING ALL THESE PLASTIC BAGS AWAY.
JELLYFISH ARE A MUCH BETTER
BREAKFAST FOR YOU.

REST WELL, BLUE.
I'LL SEE YOU TOMORROW.

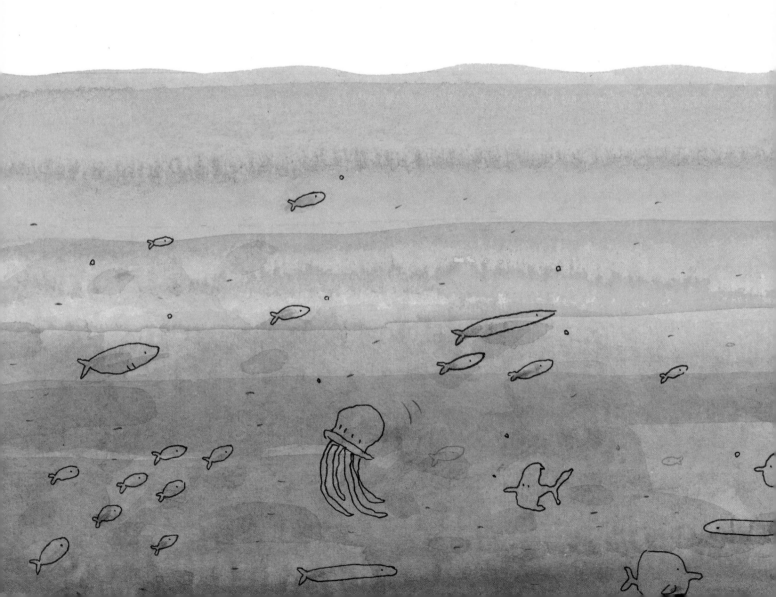

TRA LA LA! IT'S A LOVELY NEW DAY.

BLUE, WHERE ARE YOU?
DID SOMETHING HAPPEN?
BLUE?

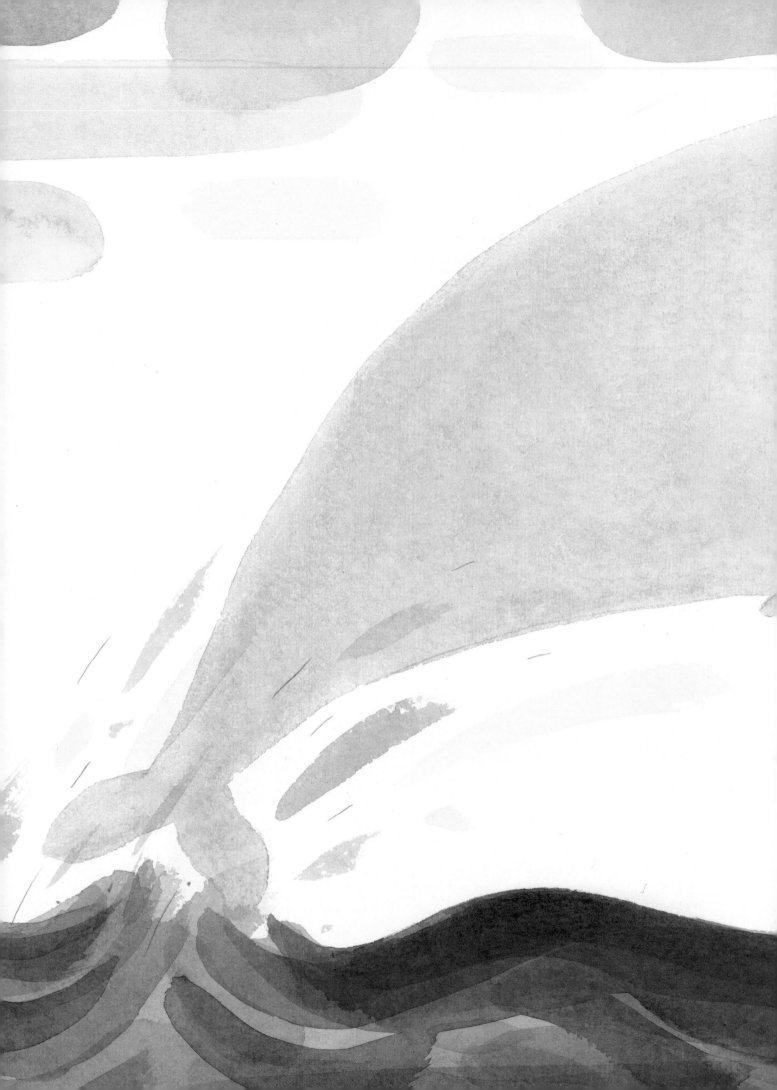

I LOVE YOU, BLUE!

SAVE OUR OCEANS.
SAVE OUR WHALES.

SAVE OUR OCEANS, SAVE OUR WHALES
A NOTE FROM BARROUX

Blue represents every kind of whale: blue whales, humpback whales, sperm whales, and many others. There are more than twenty different whale species in the world's oceans. Without our protection, many are in danger of disappearing. These great sea mammals have been overhunted by humans for centuries. Some are now protected by international laws or agreements. But all whales face another deadly threat from humans: plastic.

There are huge amounts of plastic waste in the oceans, with more added every minute. Even blue whales, which strain their food through a mesh inside their mouths, take in millions of tiny plastic particles. Sperm whales and other toothed whales swallow whole plastic bags, mistaking them for food, and are killed by the buildup of plastic waste in their bodies.

Even plastics thrown away far from any beach can end up in the ocean, which means that many people endanger whales like Blue without realizing it. Changing the habits that damage the seas can protect whales and all sea life. Here are five ways everyone can help:

- Drink from reusable containers instead of plastic bottles. Most plastic bottles are used once and can stay intact for 450 years.
- Make sure that the fish you eat come only from sustainable species. The Monterey Bay Aquarium's Seafood Watch program has a list of sustainable seafood on their app and at **www.seafoodwatch.org**.
- Try to avoid using throwaway plastic items like cups, dishes, and straws.
- Organize a plastic collection day with your family and friends.
- Buy fewer products packaged in plastic and recycle all you can. Research which types of plastic can be recycled and which cannot.

Want to learn more or volunteer to help? Here are a few organizations you can join:

- Whale and Dolphin Conservation (WDC) is a global charity with a dedicated site for children: **www.wdcs.org**.
- Save the Whales is a California-based charity focused on what young people can do: **www.savethewhales.org**.
- Surfrider is a California-based foundation working to protect the ocean from pollution, offshore drilling, and other threats: **www.surfrider.org**.